ELECTRIC ZOMBIE

LURCHING TO THE BEAT

Calico
An Imprint of Magic Wagon
abdobooks.com

by Johanna Gohmann   illustrated by Aleksandar Zolotić

FOR FLETCHER, SULLY, AND OLIVE. YOUR PARENTS
HAVE DELICIOUS BRAAAAINS. —JG

TO MY BABY SON VASILIJE, WHOSE MIDNIGHT
SCREAMS KEPT ME WORKING UNTIL DAWN. —AZ

abdobooks.com

Published by Magic Wagon, a division of ABDO, PO Box 398166,
Minneapolis, Minnesota 55439. Copyright © 2019 by Abdo
Consulting Group, Inc. International copyrights reserved in all
countries. No part of this book may be reproduced in any form
without written permission from the publisher. Calico™ is
a trademark and logo of Magic Wagon.

Printed in the United States of America, North Mankato, Minnesota.
092018
012019

 **THIS BOOK CONTAINS
RECYCLED MATERIALS**

Written by Johanna Gohmann
Illustrated by Aleksandar Zolotić
Edited by Bridget O'Brien
Art Directed by Christina Doffing

Library of Congress Control Number: 2018947811

Publisher's Cataloging-in-Publication Data

Names: Gohmann, Johanna, author. | Zolotić, Aleksandar, illustrator.
Title: Lurching to the beat / by Johanna Gohmann; illustrated by Aleksandar Zolotić.
Description: Minneapolis, Minnesota : Magic Wagon, 2019. | Series: Electric zombie; book 1
Summary: Fab and his friends think they've found the perfect drummer for their rock
    band in his new neighbor, Zee, but Zee's attire and behavior makes Fab wonder if
    his amazing drummer is really a zombie.
Identifiers: ISBN 9781532133619 (lib. bdg.) | ISBN 9781532134210 (ebook) | ISBN
    9781532134517 (Read-to-me ebook)
Subjects: LCSH: Rock groups--Juvenile fiction. | Drummers (Musicians)--Juvenile
    fiction. | First impression (Psychology)--Juvenile fiction. | Zombies--Juvenile
    fiction.
Classification: DDC [FIC]--dc23

TABLE OF CONTENTS

CHAPTER 1
BOTTLE ROCKETS 'N' BIFOCALS

Fabian Starr sits in his garage plucking at the strings of his red guitar. He gazes up at the full moon.

"I want to rock out . . . beneath a giant moon . . . like a summer werewolf . . . wearing shorts in June . . ." He sings quietly.

Beside him, his friend Emilio snorts. "Uh, Fab? What in the world is a 'summer werewolf'? And since when do werewolves wear shorts?"

"Songwriting is a process, my friend," Fab explains.

"Right," Emilio says distractedly. He picks up a wrench and tightens the bolts on an oddly shaped box.

"Writing a song is like inventing. You have to let your mind roam. Surely that's something you can relate to, Mr. Junior Engineer."

"Whatever you say, Mr. Junior Rock Star," Emilio says, frowning at the contraption at his feet.

"Something's wrong. I don't understand why it isn't launching the bottle rockets when I step on the trigger." Emilio pumps his foot over a small pedal in frustration.

"Tell me again why can't you just light the bottle rockets like a normal person?" Fab asks.

"Because that's boring, that's why!" Emilio says. He hunches over the box and fiddles with it some more.

Fab peers into the thick, dark woods across the street. The wind shakes the trees, and branches scrape toward the sky like long claws.

"You should probably head home soon," Fab says. "It's getting late."

"Not until I get this thing working," Emilio says.

Fab pushes his shaggy brown hair out of his eyes, and continues to strum his guitar. He plucks a few off-sounding notes.

"You're making my ears bleed," Emilio teases him.

"Sorry. I'm having trouble seeing in the dark," Fab says.

"You mean you're having trouble seeing without your glasses!"

"Whatever. Everyone knows rock stars don't wear bifocals." Fab shrugs.

"You're going to have trouble becoming a rock star if you can't see your guitar."

"Nope. I'm destined to become a rock star," Fab says. "With a name like Fabian Starr I kind of have to be. What else am I going to be? Fab Starr, plumber?"

"Considering we're only thirteen, I don't think you need to worry about your future career just yet," Emilio replies.

"If you and Lola would just form a band with me—"

"Fab, I already told you. I don't want to be in a rock band!" Emilio sighs. He pulls his ball cap tighter over his head, but his black curls still escape out the sides. "I am all about this . . ." He points to the picture on his hat. It's a drawing of a robot shooting flames out of its eyes.

"Killer robots?" Fab asks.

"Machines and explosions."

Just then, a black van pulls up the quiet street. It parks in front of the house directly opposite Fab's. The side of the van reads *Mr. Fleshman's Moving Company.*

"No way. Someone's finally moving into that old house?" Emilio whispers.

"Mr. Fleshman?" Fab says. "What kind of weird name is that?"

"Even weirder . . . who moves in at night?" Emilio asks.

The boys watch as three figures emerge from the van. A man, a woman, and a teenage boy.

"Do you think he's our age?" Fab whispers.

"I think he's older. But hard to tell in the dark. Am I seeing things, or are they all wearing sunglasses?"

The family of three head up the path to the front door of the house. But the way they move seems...odd.

They are walking so slowly. They must be tired, Fab thinks. *Must have been traveling all day.*

"You have got yourself some interesting new neighbors. You lucky—WHOOPS!"

Emilio accidentally steps on the pedal at his feet and his bottle rocket launcher blazes to life. Before they can stop it, a bottle rocket flies across the street and it hits the boy in the back!

"Oh no!" Fab and Emilio shout.

"You okay?" Emilio calls to the boy.

Bizarrely, the boy's parents don't even bother to turn around. They just keep lurching their way into the house. Meanwhile, the boy doesn't even flinch from the bottle rocket sticking out of his back.

"What in the world..." Fab mutters.

"Oh look!" Emilio says, pointing. "He's wearing a backpack. It only hit his pack. Whew!"

Fab peers across at the boy, and it does look like he's taking off a backpack.

"Sorry about that!" Emilio calls over. Then he bends down and busies himself with turning off his launcher.

Fab continues to watch the strange boy. He doesn't ever acknowledge Fab or Emilio. He just moves slowly into the house. *Wait a second . . .* Fab squints.

"Emilio . . ." Fab whispers. "Why does it look like the bottle rocket is still sticking out of his back?"

"Huh?" Emilio glances back up. But the door of the house is already closing, and the boy is gone.

Emilio laughs. "My friend, I'm telling you for the last time. You need to wear your glasses!"

CHAPTER 2

ROCK BAND

"I will never understand why you insist on ruining perfectly good food with that stuff." Fab shakes his head as Lola squeezes a bottle of sriracha over her taco.

"Because I like my food to hurt me a little. Try some!" Lola says. She dangles the bottle over Fab's taco, but he swats her hand away.

"Actually, I don't think it's possible to ruin these tacos," Emilio says. "This taco truck should be given every food award in existence."

"Agreed!" Fab mumbles, shoving almost an entire taco into his mouth at once.

Lola shakes her head at him. "Please don't choke. I'm too tired to do the Heimlich right now."

"Early swim practice again today, Lo?" Emilio asks.

Lola flops on the overgrown grass of the park and gives an exhausted

groan. "Ugh. Early swim every day. I *so* want to take a break from it this year!"

Fab swallows his food, and suddenly hops to his feet. "And you *should* give it a break, Lola! It's a brand-new school year. Why not try something new?"

Lola looks up at him suspiciously. "Like what?"

"Like form a rock band with your awesome friend Fab!" Fab grins.

"Ughhh . . ." Emilio and Lola both groan.

"Come *on*, you guys. It'll be awesome. Me on lead guitar, Lola on bass, Emilio on keyboard."

"Fab," Lola sighs. "Even if I did quit swim, I still have cello. I don't have time!"

"You don't have cello every day. And your cello skills are why you'll be such an awesome bassist. Not to mention the fact that you already look like a rocker with those green streaks in your hair."

Lola sits up in a huff. "For your information, Fabian Starr, my green hair is from the stupid chlorine in the pool! Does it really look green? I didn't think it was that noticeable."

"Oh." Fab grimaces. "I didn't realize. Well . . . it looks super cool on you."

Emilio lets out a snicker.

"And you," Fab says, giving Emilio's feet a kick, "are going to rock the synthesizer."

"I haven't taken piano in years, my friend. Also, I don't own a synthesizer."

"You're good enough. And with your tech skills you can probably build a synthesizer in your sleep if you want to," Fab says.

"True. But who says I want to?"

"Not only that . . . you could also build some sick pyrotechnics and special effects for our shows."

Emilio sits up. "Pyrotechnics, you say?" he asks.

"I had a feeling that would get your interest."

"I'll admit, that part sounds cool," Emilio says.

"C'mon you guys," Fab says. "What have we got to lose?"

"Our dignity?" Emilio mutters.

Lola plucks at the grass at her feet. "It would be nice to have an excuse to quit swim for a while."

"And it's always nice to have an excuse to build more explosives." Emilio scratches his chin. "But . . . I don't know. What if we suck?"

Fab flops down beside them. "I tell you what. Try it for one month. And if you seriously hate it, then I'll . . ."

"Yes?" Lola raises her eyebrows.

"I'll . . . buy you both tacos for an entire month!"

"Yes! Now you're talking!" Emilio whoops.

"But you have to try it for a full month," Fab says.

"Fine. I'm in," Emilio says. Lola nods.

"Yes!" Fab pumps his fist at the sky. "Now, just one last thing to do."

"What's that?" Lola asks.

Fab picks up two twigs and pounds them against the ground.

"Why, find a drummer of course."

CHAPTER 3

GHOST DRUMMER

"Lola, I told you. You have to wait for Emilio to kick in on keys before you start the bass line!"

Fab stands in his garage clutching his guitar. He runs his hand through his hair in frustration, and the sweat makes his shaggy locks stand up.

"I *know*. And I told *you* that it's hard to keep a beat without a drummer!"

"And I told *both* of you that I knew we would suck, and I was right!" Emilio slaps at the keys of the synthesizer.

Fab sighs. "Let's just start it from the top."

"Maybe Emilio is right." Lola plops down into a lawn chair and pulls her long greenish blond hair into a ponytail. "Maybe we just aren't very good."

"It's only our third practice!"

"Yeah, our third practice, and we still have ghost drummer over there!"

Lola complains. She gestures to the unmanned drum set sitting in the middle of the garage.

"For real, Fab. We need someone on skins," Emilio says.

"Skins, Emilio? Seriously?" Lola rolls her eyes.

"What? That's what they call the drums. I think?" Emilio scrunches his hat over his sweaty curls and heads toward the mini-fridge.

"Halt, Emilio! It's not time for a break yet. And yes, I know we need a drummer. I thought for sure my cousin could do it, but his mom said he's too busy with chess club."

"Yeah. I'm pretty sure Dave Grohl's mom said the same thing," Lola says. Emilio snorts with laughter.

"I promise I'll find someone soon." Fab sighs. "C'mon, one more time. Then we can take a break and maybe brainstorm more band names."

Lola makes a face. But she stands up and straps on her guitar.

"Wait, which key does it say to start in again?" Fab squints at the music sheet taped to the wall.

"Would you *please* just put on your glasses?" Emilio sighs.

Fab ignores him. "One. Two. One, two, three, four!"

He carefully strums the opening chord, then Emilio comes in on keyboard. He nods at Lola, and she begins her bass line.

The song is actually going okay! They've finally caught the beat.

But . . . wait, why does it sound like someone is drumming along? Fab glances around in confusion. He suddenly stops.

"Why did you quit?" Emilio shouts. "We finally had it!" He lays his face on top of the keyboard and it emits an off-key groan.

"Ssssh!" Fab waves to him. "Did you guys hear that?" Fab asks.

"Hear us finally not sucking for about four seconds, you mean?" Lola says.

"No, I thought I heard someone drumming." Fab walks to the edge of the garage and listens. But now the only thing he can hear is someone hammering.

"I think it was just your neighbor. Our old friend Bottle Rocket in the Back. See?" Emilio jerks his chin toward the house across the street.

Fab peers out of the garage and sees Emilio is right. It's the boy next door. He's standing on his porch hammering at something. He's wearing a black hoodie, dark sunglasses, and red leather gloves.

"What kind of handyman getup is that?" Lola asks.

"He wears that every day. And his parents wear the same sunglasses."

"For real?" Lola asks.

"Yeah." Fab shrugs. "Apparently they're from some tiny town in Iceland?"

"Iceland! Wow." Lola clucks her tongue.

"Yeah. I guess it's some Icelandic fashion thing or something?"

"Huh. What's his name?" Lola asks.

"He goes by Zee," Fab says. "He's a little older than us. In high school."

Suddenly, as if feeling their eyes on him, the figure across the street slowly stands.

Zee stares at the three of them. Or at least it looks like it. It's hard to tell with his sunglasses. He turns and walks slowly into his house.

"He seems kind of . . . different," Lola says.

"Yeah," Fab agrees. "My mom took some cookies over to welcome them, and he just kind of opened the door a crack, then asked her if the cookies had any meat in them."

"Meat?" Emilio makes a face.

"Are they vegetarians or something?" Lola asks.

"I don't think so," Fab says. "My mom said it kind of sounded like he was hoping there *was* meat in the cookies."

"Hmm. Maybe meat cookies are some kind of Icelandic specialty?" Lola wonders.

"Maybe," Fab says.

"Oh man," Emilio suddenly shouts. "That's it!"

Fab and Lola look at him in confusion.

"That's totally the perfect name for our band! Meat Cookie!" Emilio dances his fingers over the keyboard. "You're welcome!"

CHAPTER 4

ROCK GOD VS. THE BIG KIDS

"I'll hang these up in here, and you sneak some into the high school wing." Lola shoves a handful of flyers at Fab.

"Why don't you do the high school wing?" Fab asks nervously.

"Wait. Is Fabian Starr, rock god, afraid of the big kids?" Lola gives him a teasing smile.

"No!" Fab rolls his eyes. "I just . . . you know. Don't know their hallway that well."

"Well, I'm pretty sure it has walls, just like this one. Anyway, the flyers were your idea, remember?"

"I know." Fab sighs. "Thanks again for making them." He glances down at the stack of paper.

WANTED, it reads. *A drummer to join an awesome new band! Auditions: Thursday, 5 p.m.* Underneath was Fab's address and a drawing of a yeti playing the drums.

"Cool yeti," Fab says.

"I think The Sweaty Yetis is a better name than Meat Cookie. I'm not giving up on that. Alright, let's hurry before the bell rings."

Lola heads off down the hall and tapes a flyer above a water fountain.

Fab gives his backpack a nervous tug, then slowly pushes through the doors to the high school wing. The hall is empty except for a few stragglers making their way to class. He stands for a moment, unsure of where to start.

He decides on the vending machine, and saunters over, trying to look like he belongs. He carefully begins to tape a flyer to the front of the machine.

"How will I know if they're out of my favorite cookies if you cover it with paper?" a voice suddenly says.

"Huh?" Fab drops the scotch tape. It slides under the vending machine. He turns and sees an older girl with purple-streaked hair and green eyes.

"You lost your tape." She smiles.

"Oh. Yeah." Fab crouches down and peers under the machine.

"Looking for a drummer, huh?" He stands and sees her reading the flyer.

"Yeah." He clears his throat. "Trying to get a band going."

"Wait, are you Fab?"

"I am!" He leans against the wall in what he hopes is a cool pose. "How did you know?"

"I heard my cousin Lola talk about you," she says.

"Oh right," Fab says. "You're Josie. Lola's mentioned you. You just moved here from Brooklyn, right?"

"Yep." Josie gives him another smile. "Really cool you're forming a band. I used to go see my friends in Brooklyn play all the time."

"Oh man, there's so much great music in Brooklyn! I mean, that's what I hear, anyway," Fab says.

"Totally." Josie nods. "Well, I better get to class. Good luck finding your tape." She heads off down the hall, then suddenly stops. She turns around. "Hey, what's your band called, by the way?"

Fab stares at her blankly for a moment. "Um. Meat Cookie?" he mumbles.

Josie wrinkles her nose. "Hmm. Might want to work on that name," she says.

Fab can feel his face go red, and quickly kneels down. He focuses on getting the scotch tape out from under the vending machine.

CHAPTER 5

THE AUDITION BLUES

"You guys ready to find our new drummer?" Fab gives the drum a loud smack. It's Thursday afternoon, and Lola, Emilio, and he are in his garage.

"But I still don't understand. Why would anyone want to shoot paintballs from their skateboard?" Lola says. Emilio is busy showing off his latest invention.

"Think about the cool designs you can make while you're skating! It'll be like a new art form. The balls shoot out of this tube, see? And then—"

"Emilio!" Fab shouts. "Enough with your painting skateboard! Here come some people."

They watch as two figures make their way toward the garage. One is a tall, thin girl with a long braid. She wears a prim, flowered dress and a very serious expression.

The other is Todd Brick, a muscular boy Fab recognizes from gym class, and who's known for throwing the dodgeball so hard it leaves a mark.

"Hi guys!" Fab smiles. "Welcome! So, um . . . is there anyone else behind you two?"

"No," the tall girl says.

"Really?" Fab asks, trying to hide his disappointment.

"Really," the girl says flatly.

"Right." Fab nods. "Okay, let's get started then. Who wants to audition first?"

No one moves.

"I'll go." Todd Brick shrugs.

He makes his way over to the drum set and squeezes his muscular body onto the little stool. He picks up the sticks and begins to bang and thrash away.

There doesn't appear to be any rhythm to what he's playing. It's just really loud and angry sounding.

"He plays drums like he plays dodgeball," Emilio whispers to Fab.

Fab lets Todd bash away for a few seconds, then waves his hands in the air. "Thank you!" Fab shouts. "Thanks Todd!"

Todd at last stops his rampage.

"So, um. How long have you been playing drums?" Fab asks.

"This is my first time, actually," Todd says. "I just wanted to try it. I had a feeling I'd be good."

"I see," Fab mutters.

"It's not as fun as I thought it'd be though." Todd scratches his back with a stick. "My mom's making turkey burgers. See you later." He picks up his bag and jogs out of the garage.

Fab glances over at Lola. She's struggling not to burst out laughing.

Fab turns to the girl. "Well! Looks like you're next! Sorry, what's your name?"

"Beatrice? I sit right behind you in algebra, Fab." She eyes him stonily. Fab hears Lola muffle another giggle.

"Beatrice. Of course," Fab says. "Please, go ahead!"

Beatrice sits on the drum stool, carefully positioning her long, flowered dress over the top of it. She daintily picks up the sticks.

Then she launches into a furious, thrashing rhythm, her long braid swings wildly behind her. To Fab's surprise, she's actually not bad! She plays for a couple of minutes, then sedately puts the sticks on top of the snare.

Fab smiles at her. "Where did you learn to do that?"

"I play drums in my church group," Beatrice says.

"Your church must really rock out," Lola says.

"Oh no." Beatrice shakes her head. "They only play hymns. But I like metal. You guys play metal, right?"

"Uh, no, actually," Fab mumbles. "We're more . . . regular rock."

"Seriously?" Beatrice gives them a disdainful look. "Ugh. No thanks then. I only want to be in a metal band." And with that, she smooths her skirt down and walks out.

As soon as she's gone, Fab hits the button to close the garage door. Once it's fully shut, he turns to Emilio and Lola, a baffled look on his face.

"That was interesting," Lola says.

"That's one word for it." Emilio smirks, then immediately goes back to fidgeting with his skateboard again.

"Emilio!" Fab shouts, sounding a bit angrier than he means to. "If you explode a paintball in my mom's garage I'm going to decimate you!"

"Hey! Don't be mad at me just because the auditions were a bust," Emilio says.

"Sorry, Fab." Lola gives his shoulder a pat. "I can't believe only two people showed."

Fab flops dejectedly into a lawn chair, keeping his eyes on Emilio.

"I mean it, dude!" he shouts again.

"Fab, will you relax? The paintballs don't eject unless you pop the board a certain way and—"

BAM! A paintball fires out of the back of Emilio's board, and red paint explodes on the wall directly behind the drum set.

"Oops." Emilio looks at Fab nervously.

Fab watches the paint ooze down the wall. He puts his face in his hands.

"I thought it was in off mode! I'll totally repaint the wall, I promise!"

"Oh, whatever. I don't care about the wall." Fab sighs. "I can't believe it's this hard to find a stupid drummer. I mean what kind of deal with the devil do we need to make?"

Suddenly, there's a sharp knock on the garage door. They freeze, staring at each other.

"Do you think . . . someone else showed?" Lola whispers.

"It's probably just my mom checking in," Fab whispers back.

"Only one way to find out!" Emilio hits the button on the garage door. It

slowly rises, revealing a lone, hooded
figure.

A sunset blazes in the distance,
and in its glare, all they can make out
is the dark silhouette of a boy.

A boy, Fab is happy to note, who is carrying drumsticks. Fab squints. He's also wearing dark sunglasses and red leather gloves.

Zee.

CHAPTER 6

DEAL WITH THE DEVIL

Fab stands, using a hand to shield his eyes from the sun. "Hi. You're Zee, right? I'm Fab." Zee says nothing.

"Welcome to the neighborhood! Um . . . I don't think we've had a chance to meet yet. This is Lola." Lola gives a small wave. "She plays bass," Fab says. "And this is Emilio. He's on keyboard."

"Hey." Emilio walks over. "Hope your backpack is okay! From . . . the other night. That was an accident."

Zee says nothing. He just stands there. His face is incredibly pale, and his mouth sits in a straight line.

"So . . . uh . . . did you want to audition?" Fab gestures uncertainly to Zee's drumsticks.

Zee still says nothing. But slowly . . . *very, very slowly* . . . begins to make his way to the drums. *Why does he move like he's underwater?* Fab wonders.

Emilio leans over to whisper into Fab's ear. "He's perfect if we only want to play slow songs."

Zee stops in his tracks. He stares at the red ooze dripping down the wall.

"Sorry about the mess," Fab says. "Another one of Emilio's accidents."

"Sorry it looks like a crime scene." Emilio chuckles. "Our last drummer was so bad we had to kill him!"

Zee turns his head slowly to the side. "You did?" he whispers.

For a moment, no one says anything.

"Uh. N-no," Emilio stammers. "That was . . . a joke."

Zee nods, then positions himself behind the drum set. Emilio shoots Fab a look, but Fab just shrugs.

Finally, at last, Zee is seated. He holds up the drumsticks, and ever

so slowly taps them together three times. He then launches into one of the fastest, coolest drum solos Fab has ever heard.

Zee's arms absolutely *fly* over the drums. His red gloves flash as he pounds and thrashes at the set.

Fab can't believe it! He looks at his friends. Both of their mouths are hanging open.

He then realizes his *own* mouth is hanging open. Zee really is unbelievable!

After a few electrifying minutes, Zee stops.

"Wow! That was amazing!" Fab can't control himself. He's so excited he wants to jump up and hug him.

Zee says nothing. Just slowly stands. The drumming over, he's now back to moving in his weird, lurchy fashion. He turns and again looks at the mess on the wall.

"You know . . ." he suddenly says. He has a quiet voice, and an odd sounding accent that Fab has never heard before. *Icelandic*, Fab thinks.

"What?" Fab says.

"It okay to kill bad drummers," Zee says. "The world not need more bad drummers."

He slowly reaches out and touches the red ooze. He then brings his hand up to his mouth as if to taste it. Lola, Emilio, and Fab stare, their eyes wide.

Zee gives them a tiny smile. "That also joke," he says.

"Oh!" Fab says. "Of course. Ha!"

Zee watches them for a moment. "So," he says. "I am in band?"

Fab looks at Lola and Emilio. Lola's eyebrows are arched so high on her face they look like they might fly off her skull. And Emilio's expression is like someone who just swallowed a bug.

But Fab can't stop grinning.

"Yes!" he shouts. "Yes. You are totally in the band."

He reaches out to shake one of Zee's gloved hands. But Zee just stands there, holding his sticks.

"Cool," he says. And his mouth forms another tiny, almost imperceptible smile.

CHAPTER 7

PARTY OF PRINCESSES

Fab and Zee stand in line at the taco truck. They've just finished their second practice as a new band, and Fab can't believe how much better they sound with Zee. He suggested they go for a taco run to celebrate.

Behind him, he can hear Lola and Emilio debating the merits of hard shells versus soft shells. Fab glances at Zee. His neighbor isn't much of a talker, he's noticed.

Fab clears his throat, and tries to think of something to say. "So . . . um. Do you miss Iceland?" Fab asks.

"Yes," Zee mumbles.

"Yeah. I guess it's pretty different here," Fab says. Zee says nothing. Just adjusts his sunglasses slightly.

"Alright kids, what can I get you?" The waitress at the window leans out to them.

"Three fish tacos, please," Fab says.

"And you?" the waitress asks Zee.

"One raw chicken taco, if you please," Zee says.

The waitress stares at Zee. "Pardon?"

"One raw chicken taco. No lettuce," Zee says.

The waitress gives Fab a look, and Fab can hear Emilio snicker.

"I don't know what kind of prank this is, kids. But I can't give you raw chicken. That's a health violation."

Fab glances at Zee, and he swears it looks like a small blush is creeping into Zee's incredibly pale cheeks.

"Is cooked chicken okay, buddy?" Fab asks.

Zee just nods, then slowly lurches away.

Fab brings their food to their usual spot in the grass where they stuff their faces. Lola wipes sauce on a napkin and claps her hands together.

"I have some exciting news!" She smiles. "My little sister is turning six next week, right? And she's throwing this big princess party . . ."

"Ooh! Yay!" Emilio squeals. "Princesses!"

Fab laughs, but Lola rolls her eyes.

"And . . . I convinced my mom to hire us as the entertainment! The Sweaty Yetis have their first gig!"

"Wait. What?" Fab sits up.

"Yeah, first of all, we're called Meat Cookie. And secondly, you booked us at a six-year-old's princess party? Are you nuts?" Emilio says.

"We have to start somewhere," Lola says. "And this is perfect, because if we stink, who cares?"

"I don't know, Lo . . ." Fab says. "That's not much time."

"The practice will be good for us. Plus, my cousin Josie from Brooklyn will be there, and she's been to tons of concerts. She can give us tips!"

Fab chews on his lip. On one hand, the idea of performing at a princess party sounds humiliating.

But on the other, the idea of performing in front of Josie . . . he isn't sure if this makes him want to throw up or cheer.

Fab turns to Zee. Zee's fifteen. A high schooler. He might think the idea of rocking out at a princess party is beyond ridiculous. "Zee," Fab says. "What do you think?"

Zee ever so slowly pulls himself to his feet. He turns and points at Lola. "You."

Lola looks at him in surprise. "Yes?"

"You make hair more green. Not green enough for rock and roll." He flips his hood over his head. "As for the party of princesses . . . We do it," he says.

He then begins his slow lurch away, making his way across the park toward home.

They stare after him. "Uh, goodbye to you, too, Zee." Lola turns to Fab, a bewildered look on her face.

"Alright." Fab smiles. "I guess we're doing it!"

"Wait, what? The weirdo gets to decide?" Emilio says.

"Don't call him a weirdo," Fab says.

"Raw chicken, Fab? You don't think raw chicken is weird?" Emilio makes a face.

"It's probably an Icelandic thing!" Fab says. "In France they eat steak tartare, which is raw meat."

"Right." Emilio scoffs. "And the fact that he can play drums like lightning, but then moves like a sloth the rest of the time? Is that also an Icelandic tradition?"

"He is a little odd, Fab," Lola says. "He hardly ever talks."

"He's just shy!" Fab says. "And anyway, who cares? He's an amazing drummer. So what if he's a bit of a loner? Most great musicians are loners."

"I suppose . . ." Lola fiddles with her shoelaces.

"It'll be great. I'm psyched! Thanks for booking the gig, Lo." Fab smiles and takes a final gulp of his soda.

Emilio shakes his head. "I sure am looking forward to all the tacos you're going to have to buy us once this band falls apart."

"Oh shush." Fab playfully tosses his empty bottle at Emilio.

CHAPTER 8

SPARKLES THE MACHINE

Fab runs his hands through his sweaty hair, and as usual it stands up in all directions. They've been practicing for an hour. Everyone is exhausted. But the party is tomorrow. He wants them to sound good! Or at least, not terrible.

"Fab, I think we can call it a night," Lola says. "We're playing my little sister's birthday party, not Madison Square Garden."

"Yes," Zee says. "Arms tired. We done." Fab looks up in surprise. Zee usually seems like he can play all night.

"Okay." Fab nods. "So. Any last thoughts?"

"You." Zee suddenly points at Fab. "Tomorrow, wear hair like that. Up toward ceiling."

"What?" Fab feels his sweaty hair. "You want me to do this on purpose?"

"It more rock and roll," Zee says.

Fab starts to respond, but Emilio lugs something wrapped in a beach towel to the middle of the floor.

"Before everyone takes off, allow me to unveil my secret weapon." Emilio grins, a mischievous glint in his eyes. He whips off the towel.

"I give you, Sparkles the Unicorn!"

In the middle of the floor sits a purple unicorn made of metal and plastic. It's the size of a large dog, and has a long golden horn.

"Yes!" Lola laughs. "My sister will really like that."

"Oh, she'll more than like it," Emilio says. He walks back to his keyboard and flips a switch. A small jet of rainbow sparks shoot out of the unicorn's horn.

"Wow!" Fab and Lola shout. But there's suddenly a loud bang and clatter. Fab looks over and sees Zee is so panicked he's actually knocked over two of his drums. They all turn and stare at him.

"You okay, buddy?" Fab walks over to help him up, but Zee just brushes him off.

"I fine. I just . . . I must go help Father now." Zee heads out of the garage toward his house. They stand in confusion as he stumbles away.

"Okay! We'll see you tomorrow at 3 p.m., right?" Fab calls after him. But Zee doesn't respond. Fab notices that he doesn't go in his house. Instead he heads off to the woods behind it.

"I think that's the fastest I've ever seen him move when he isn't playing the drums," Emilio says.

"Do you think he has a firework phobia or something?" Lola says.

Fab watches as Zee disappears into the thick shadows of the woods. "Hmm. Maybe."

"Anyway, nice work, Emilio. Sparkles is awesome!" Lola starts packing up her stuff to head home.

"Thanks. I figure it will be a great distraction if we suck." Emilio grabs his backpack to follow Lola.

"Will you please stop saying we're going to suck?" Fab sighs.

"Sorry buddy. It will be great. I hope . . ." He widens his eyes and pretends to bite at his nails.

Fab jokingly shoves him out of the garage, then he watches Emilio and Lola stroll away. He turns his gaze back to the dark woods behind Zee's house.

It was pretty bizarre how shaken up Zee seemed. And Zee hardly ever mentioned his parents. *Help his dad do what?* Fab wonders.

A terrible thought occurs to him: *What if Zee decides not to show up tomorrow?* Fab imagines Josie watching as they struggle without a drummer. It makes him cringe.

Maybe he should go check on Zee? Just make sure he's okay?

Fab starts toward the woods. A chilly breeze tousles his hair, and he zips up his jacket.

He pauses at the edge of the trees. *Why would Zee go there this time of night? It's pitch-black in there.*

Fab hears a rustling sound up ahead. He takes a few steps into the woods, then a few more. He's sure he can see someone in the distance.

He moves a bit closer, and almost calls out Zee's name. But then the moon comes out from behind a cloud and casts its faint glow on the figure ahead.

Is that . . . ? Fab fumbles in his pockets for his glasses. He slips them on, and his eyes widen.

He sees what looks like Zee's dad pushing a wheelbarrow . . . a wheelbarrow overflowing with different dead animals! Coyotes, a cat, some birds. Their eyes are all black and lifeless. *What the . . . ?*

Behind him, Fab hears a twig snap. He freezes. Someone is there. His heart pounds in his ears. He turns and races out of the woods, back toward the safety of home.

CHAPTER 9

LET'S ROCK THESE PRINCESSES

The next day, Fab and Emilio stand on Lola's porch, waiting to be let in. "Interesting hairdo, Fab."

Fab pats at his spiky hair. He had to borrow some of his mom's hair goop to get it to stand straight up. "It's just for the gig. Does it look stupid?"

"Not if you're going to a porcupine convention." Emilio grins.

Suddenly the front door swings open. Fab and Emilio gasp. Lola's hair is the color of spinach.

"Whoa!" Emilio shouts. "Is this National Bonkers Hair Day or what?"

Lola blushes slightly. "I decided Zee was right. I needed to commit to the color, you know?"

"It looks awesome!" Fab says.

Lola grins. "Yours does too."

"It's such a cool shade of green!" Fab says.

"Thanks. Josie did it for me. She's really good at that stuff."

"Josie's here?" Fab gulps.

"In the back. How did you guys sleep? I tossed and turned all night!"

Fab says nothing. He hasn't told them about the episode in the woods. He still isn't sure what he saw. And he doesn't want to give them another reason to think Zee is a weirdo.

"I couldn't sleep either!" Emilio says. "I feel like a total zombie."

Fab suddenly looks at his friend. A small thought nags at his brain. "You feel like a what?"

"Like a—"

"Hi kids." Lola's mom appears in the doorway. "You ready? The girls are so excited. Follow me."

"How in the world did I let you talk me into this?" Emilio mutters.

Fab and Emilio stand in Lola's backyard. A dozen little girls in princess costumes run around shrieking and laughing. A bag of balloons is tied in a tree.

A group of parents stand near a refreshment table. Fab sees Josie's purple head leaning over to help position candles on a cake.

"My mom said we could use the deck as a stage. Do you guys want to start setting up?" Lola says.

"Sure," Fab says, his palms glazed in sweat. "Any sign of Zee?"

"He didn't come with you guys?" Lola cocks her head in surprise. "Huh. I'm sure he'll be here soon. Let's get our gear!"

Fab and Emilio have set up the instruments and speakers, and even positioned Sparkles at the side of the stage. But still no sign of Zee. The little girls and adults are staring up at them expectantly. Fab's stomach is in knots.

"Where *is* he?" Emilio growls in Fab's ear. "I feel like the princesses are going to attack if we don't play soon!"

"He's only a few minutes late." Fab tries to sound calm.

"There he is!" Lola suddenly shouts with relief.

Fab looks up and sees Zee's familiar black hoodie and sunglasses. He lurches onto the deck.

"I so sorry I late!" he says.

"It's alright. Glad you're here now."
Fab smiles anxiously.

Zee looks at him. "You are nervous."

"Maybe a little," Fab mumbles.
"Yeah."

"Do not be," Zee says softly. "Trust
me. We are going to rock these
princesses."

He suddenly leans close to Fab's
face, and for the first time ever, he
lifts his sunglasses slightly.

Fab tries not to flinch at his eyes.
They are the most yellowish shade
of green he's ever seen. Zee winks

one greenish eye, then swiftly drops his sunglasses back down. He then lurches over to his position behind the drums.

Fab glances at his friends. They are clutching at their instruments, looking as nervous as he feels. He looks at Zee, and Zee gives him a small smile. Fab smiles back.

Let's rock these princesses.

He strums a chord, and they launch into their first song. The little girls stop their shrieking, and the adults stop chattering.

We sound good! Fab thinks. He looks at Lola, and she shakes her green hair in time to the beat. The little girls dance and sing along.

Fab glances at Emilio and wants to laugh at the sight. Emilio is dancing behind his keyboard with a huge grin on his face.

When they finish the song, the adults clap. The little girls point their glittery wands at the stage. "More music! More music!" they chant.

They play two more songs. By the end of the final number, the crowd is clapping along. Fab's hair is standing in a million sweaty directions as he belts the last line of the song.

He turns to watch Zee, who is supposed to end the set with a solo. The crowd cheers as Zee's gloves fly over the drums. He's killing it!

Zee pounds his way into the final beats. Emilio flips the switch on his keyboard, and rainbow sparks shoot from the unicorn. The little girls shriek in delight. At the same time, Lola's mom releases the balloons tied up in the tree.

In all the commotion, Fab watches as Zee pounds out the final beat. As the balloons drift down around him, Fab's jaw drops.

Did he just see what he thought he saw? Fab rubs at his eyes. He of course isn't wearing his glasses. But

. . . he's sure he saw it! He saw Zee's hand fly off!

Fab stands frozen. He knows he saw something red fly off the end of Zee's wrist.

It was probably just one of the balloons, Fab! Get a grip! he tells himself. *Or maybe it was just one of his gloves?*

He stares over at Zee. Zee now has his hands jammed tightly into his hoodie pockets.

The crowd cheers, and Fab hears Josie call up from the back. "You forgot to tell us your name! Say the name of the band!"

Fab pauses. He glances at Zee. And suddenly, he knows exactly just what to say.

"We're called Electric Zombie!" he shouts into the mic. The crowd cheers, and Lola and Emilio look at him, clearly confused by the name.

But there's something about the way Zee nods ever so slightly under his hoodie. He seems to understand perfectly well.

CHAPTER 10
PLATES, CAKE + FANFARE

The band stands near the refreshment table. A group of little girls swarms around them excitedly.

"You guys are real rock stars!" one princess says breathlessly.

"Thanks!" Fab smiles.

"Can I have your autograph?" she asks, holding up a crayon. Another little girl shoves her to the side.

"It's my birthday, so I get his autograph first!" Lola's little sister Katie holds up a paper plate for him to sign.

"My pleasure, Katie," Fab says. "Are you having a good birthday?"

"Yes," she says shyly. She pulls off her pink tiara and puts it on his head. "You get to wear my special tiara because you were the best one!"

"I shall wear it with pride."

Lola snaps his photo with her phone. "For the cover of *Rolling Stone*," she teases.

"Hey, what do you mean he was the best one?" Emilio pretends to be hurt. "I'm the one who built Sparkles the Unicorn!"

"Really? I'll take your autograph too, then." Katie holds her paper plate out to Emilio.

Just then, Josie appears at Fab's side. "You guys were amazing!" she says.

"You think so?" Fab beams.

"Totally! I was just saying to Lola that you should audition to play the middle school fair."

"You think we're ready for something like that?" Fab says.

"More than ready. Especially with such an awesome drummer." Josie smiles at Zee, who is standing quietly off to the side.

"I'm Josie, Lola's cousin." She holds her hand out to shake, and Fab watches Zee closely. He keeps his hands firmly jammed into his pockets.

"Nice to meet," he says. "In my country we no shake hands. We bump elbows." He holds out his

elbow for Josie to bump, and gives
her a small smile.

"Elbows? Um, okay." Josie laughs
and bumps her elbow against Zee's.

"Yeah, Lola told me you're from Iceland! That's so cool. You know, I just moved here too."

"Cool," Zee says quietly. He then turns, and walks slowly away, into the house. Josie watches him go, a puzzled look on her face.

"You really think we could play the middle school fair?" Fab asks her. She turns back to him.

"Oh yeah! But you might want to ditch your tiara for the auditions."

Fab brushes at the top of his head, and his face goes crimson. "Ha! I totally forgot I had this on!" He rips the tiara off.

"I better go help with the cake," Josie says. "Was great to hear you guys play, Fab. I really dig the band name. And the hair." She flashes him a smile before walking away.

Fab turns to Emilio and Lola. They are still busy autographing plates.

"What do you guys say? Ready for some middle school fair action?"

"Are you kidding? We're more than ready. We were born rock stars!" Emilio says.

"Born rock stars, eh?" Fab shakes his head. "Only one show, and how quickly you change your tune . . ."

Emilio shrugs. "It was a lot more fun than I expected."

"Agreed," Lola says. "I'm definitely up for the fair."

"Awesome! Let's go find Zee and see what he thinks," Fab says. The three of them head into the house. But Lola's mom says Zee left a few minutes ago.

They quickly run outside. Sure enough, there in the distance, they see Zee's silhouette as he lurches off into the sunset.

"What is it with this dude and his inability to say goodbye?" Emilio shakes his head.

"Should I run after him?" Fab asks.

"Yeah, he's gonna miss the cake," Emilio says.

"Nah, let him go if he wants," Lola says. "He doesn't seem like a cake person."

"Yeah," Fab says.

He tries to ignore the uneasy feeling in his stomach. Lola turns, and sees the troubled look on his face. She slings an arm over his shoulder.

"Relax, Fab. Remember, most great musicians are loners."

Fab nods. *And most zombies don't like cake,* he thinks.